Nathaniel Hawthorne

The SCARLET LETTER

adapted by

P. Craig Russell
WRITER, LAYOUT ARTIST

Jill Thompson
ARTIST

Bill Pearson
LETTERER

CLASSICS ILLUSTRATED

BERKLEY/ FIRST PUBLISHING

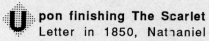

Upon finishing **The Scarlet Letter** in 1850, Nathaniel Hawthorne read the manuscript to his wife, Sophia. "It broke her heart," Hawthorne later wrote, "and sent her to bed with a grievous headache, which I look upon as a triumphant success." Although Hawthorne completed the tragic romance in a year's time, he actually had been preparing for 20 years to write his self-described "hell-fire story" of shame and redemption: his first mention of an adulteress condemned to wear a scarlet "A" came in the story *Endicott and the Red Cross*, published in 1837. **The Scarlet Letter** — which Hawthorne originally intended to be a short story but expanded at the suggestion of his publisher — displays his lifelong preoccupation with the themes of secrecy and guilt, the conflict between intellectual and moral price, and the lingering effects of Puritanism, the strict Protestant religion that flourished in New England in the 1600s. Generally regarded as the first symbolic novel to be written in the United States, **The Scarlet Letter** is peopled with characters who are meant to be the embodiments of moral traits, rather than realistic, living figures. Still, the novel abounds in rich imagery, which summons up the grim, stark lifestyle of Boston's Puritans, and the surrounding wilderness that played an important part in shaping their Utopian experiment in the New World. Among the most unified novels ever written, it is remarkable, too, for Hawthorne's painstakingly tight structure, and his rich, lyrical language. A radical departure from the realistic novels of the mid-19th century, **The Scarlet Letter** was one of the inspirations for the pre-Civil War Gothic movement in American literature.

The Scarlet Letter
Classics Illustrated, Number 6

Wade Roberts, Editorial Director
Alex Wald, Art Director

PRINTING HISTORY
1st edition published March 1990

For information, address: The Berkley Publishing Group, 200 Madison Avenue, New York, New York 10016.

ISBN 0-425-12024-4

TRADEMARK NOTICE: Classics Illustrated® is a registered trademark of Frawley Corporation. The Classics Illustrated logo is a trademark of The Berkley Publishing Group and First Publishing, Inc. "Berkley" and the stylized "B" are trademarks of The Berkley Publishing Group. "First Publishing" and the stylized "1F" are trademarks of First Publishing, Inc.

Distributed by Berkley Sales & Marketing, a division of The Berkley Publishing Group, 200 Madison Avenue, New York, New York 10016.

Printed in the United States of America
1 2 3 4 5 6 7 8 9 0

THE FOUNDERS OF A NEW COLONY, WHATEVER UTOPIA THEY MIGHT PROJECT, HAVE INVARIABLY RECOGNIZED IT AMONG THEIR EARLIEST NECESSITIES TO ALLOT A PORTION OF THE VIRGIN SOIL AS A CEMETERY, AND ANOTHER PORTION AS THE SITE OF A PRISON.

IT MAY BE ASSUMED THAT THE FOREFATHERS OF BOSTON HAD BUILT THE FIRST PRISON HOUSE ALMOST AS SEASONABLY AS THE FIRST BURIAL GROUND.

SOME FIFTEEN OR TWENTY YEARS AFTER THE SETTLEMENT OF THE TOWN, THE WOODEN JAIL WAS ALREADY MARKED WITH WEATHER-STAINS AND OTHER INDICATIONS OF AGE WHICH GAVE A YET DARKER ASPECT TO ITS BEETLE-BROWED AND GLOOMY FRONT. THE RUST ON THE PONDEROUS IRON-WORK OF ITS OAKEN DOOR LOOKED MORE ANTIQUE THAN ANYTHING ELSE IN THE NEW WORLD. LIKE ALL THAT PERTAINS TO CRIME, IT SEEMED NEVER TO HAVE KNOWN A YOUTHFUL ERA.

BUT ON ONE SIDE OF THE PORTAL, ROOTED ALMOST AT THE THRESHOLD, WAS A WILD ROSEBUSH, COVERED, IN THIS MONTH OF JUNE, WITH ITS DELICATE GEMS.

FINDING IT SO DIRECTLY ON THE THRESHOLD OF OUR NARRATIVE, WE COULD HARDLY DO OTHERWISE THAN PLUCK ONE OF ITS FLOWERS, AND PRESENT IT TO THE READER.

IT MAY SERVE, LET US HOPE, TO SYMBOLIZE SOME SWEET MORAL BLOSSOM THAT MAY BE FOUND ALONG THE TRACK, OR RELIEVE THE DARKENING CLOSE OF A TALE OF HUMAN FRAILTY AND SORROW.

THE GRASS PLOT BEFORE THE JAIL WAS OCCUPIED ON A CERTAIN SUMMER MORNING BY A LARGE NUMBER OF THE INHABITANTS OF BOSTON, ALL WITH THEIR EYES FASTENED ON THE IRON-CLAMPED OAKEN DOOR.

GOODWIVES, IF ONLY WE WOMEN OF VIRTUE SHOULD HAVE THE HANDLE OF SUCH AS THIS HESTER PRYNNE. WOULD SHE COME OFF WITH SUCH A MERCIFUL SENTENCE? MARRY, I TROW NOT!

LITTLE WILL SHE CARE WHAT THEY PUT UPON HER GOWN! SHE MAY COVER IT WITH A BROOCH, OR SUCHLIKE ADORNMENT, AND WALK THE STREETS AS BRAVE AS EVER!

THE REVEREND DIMMESDALE, HER GODLY PASTOR, TAKES IT VERY GRIEVOUSLY THAT SUCH A SCANDAL SHOULD HAVE COME UPON HIS CONGREGATION.

THEY SHOULD HAVE PUT THE BRAND OF A HOT IRON ON HER FOREHEAD.

THIS WOMAN HAS BROUGHT US SHAME, AND OUGHT TO DIE.

MERCY ON US, GOODWIFE. IS THERE NO VIRTUE, SAVE WHAT SPRINGS FROM A FEAR OF GALLOWS?

HUSH, NOW, FOR THE PRISON LOCK IS TURNING, AND HERE COMES MISTRESS PRYNNE HERSELF.

MAKE WAY, MAKE WAY! A BLESSING ON THE RIGHTEOUS COLONY OF THE MASSA-CHUSETTS, WHERE INIQUITY IS DRAGGED OUT INTO THE SUNSHINE!

COME ALONG, MADAM HESTER, AND SHOW YOUR SCARLET LETTER!

WHEN THE YOUNG WOMAN—THE MOTHER OF THE CHILD—STOOD BEFORE THE CROWD...

...IT SEEMED HER FIRST IMPULSE TO CLASP THE INFANT MORE CLOSELY TO HER BOSOM.

IN A MOMENT, HOW-EVER, JUDGING THAT ONE TOKEN OF HER SHAME WOULD POORLY SERVE TO HIDE ANOTHER, SHE TOOK THE BABY ON HER ARM, AND, WITH A BURNING BLUSH AND A HAUGHTY SMILE, LOOKED AROUND AT HER TOWNS-PEOPLE AND NEIGHBORS.

A LANE WAS OPENED THROUGH THE CROWD. HESTER PRYNNE SET FORTH TOWARDS THE PLACE APPOINTED FOR HER PUNISHMENT...

THIS SCAFFOLD WAS HELD TO BE AS EFFECTUAL AN AGENT IN THE PROMOTION OF GOOD CITIZENSHIP AS WAS THE GUILLOTINE AMONG THE TERRORISTS OF FRANCE.

...AND CAME AT LENGTH TO A SORT OF SCAFFOLD.

HESTER'S SENTENCE BORE THAT SHE SHOULD STAND A CERTAIN TIME UPON THE PLATFORM.

KNOWING HER PART, SHE ASCENDED A FLIGHT OF STEPS...

...AND WAS DISPLAYED TO THE MULTITUDE.

THE UNHAPPY CULPRIT SUSTAINED HERSELF AS BEST A WOMAN MIGHT, UNDER THE WEIGHT OF A THOUSAND UNRELENTING EYES, ALL FASTENED UPON HER AND CONCENTRATED AT HER BOSOM.

IT WAS ALMOST INTOLERABLE TO BE BORNE.

YET THERE WERE INTERVALS WHEN THE WHOLE SCENE SEEMED TO GLIMMER INDISTINCTLY, LIKE A MASS OF IMPERFECTLY SHAPED AND SPECTRAL IMAGES. REMINISCENCES CAME SWARMING BACK; ONE PICTURE PRECISELY AS VIVID AS ANOTHER.

SHE SAW AGAIN HER NATIVE VILLAGE, IN OLD ENGLAND, AND HER PATERNAL HOME.

SHE SAW HER FATHER'S FACE, WITH ITS BALD BROW AND WHITE BEARD, AND HER MOTHER'S FACE, WITH ITS LOOK OF HEEDFUL AND ANXIOUS LOVE.

SHE SAW A MAN WELL STRICKEN IN YEARS, WITH EYES DIM AND BLEARED, WHOSE FIGURE WAS SLIGHTLY DEFORMED.

SHE SAW A CITY, WHERE A NEW LIFE HAD AWAITED HER.

LASTLY, CAME THE RUDE MARKETPLACE, WITH ALL THE PURITAN TOWNSPEOPLE LEVELLING THEIR STERN REGARDS AT HESTER PRYNNE--WHO STOOD ON THE SCAFFOLD, AN INFANT IN HER ARM, AND THE LETTER "A" IN SCARLET, UPON HER BOSOM.

FROM THIS INTENSE CONSCIOUSNESS OF BEING THE OBJECT OF SEVERE AND UNIVERSAL OBSERVATION, THE WEARER OF THE SCARLET LETTER WAS RELIEVED, BY DISCERNING A FIGURE WHICH TOOK POSSESSION OF HER THOUGHTS.

I PRAY YOU, WHO IS THIS WOMAN -- AND WHERE-FORE IS SHE SET UP TO PUBLIC SHAME?

YOU MUST BE A STRANGER IN THIS REGION, ELSE YOU WOULD HAVE HEARD... SHE HATH RAISED A GREAT SCANDAL IN GODLY MASTER DIMMESDALE'S CHURCH.

TRUE, I AM A STRANGER, AND HAVE BEEN A WANDERER. I HAVE MET WITH MIS-HAPS BY SEA AND LAND. WHAT HAS BROUGHT THIS WOMAN TO YONDER SCAFFOLD?

SHE WAS THE WIFE OF A LEARNED MAN, ENGLISH BY BIRTH, WHO WAS MINDED TO CROSS OVER AND CAST HIS LOT WITH US.

HE SENT HIS WIFE BEFORE HIM, BUT... BEING LEFT TO HER OWN AFFAIRS...

AND WHO MAY BE THE FATHER OF YONDER BABE?

OF THAT MATTER, MADAM HESTER REFUSETH TO SPEAK. BUT SINCE, MOST LIKELY, HER HUSBAND IS AT THE BOTTOM OF THE SEA, THE EXTREMITY OF OUR LAW -- DEATH -- HAS NOT BEEN PUT IN FORCE.

MERCIFULLY, SHE HAS BEEN DOOMED TO STAND ONLY THREE HOURS ON THE PLATFORM, AND THEN, FOR THE REMAINDER OF HER LIFE, TO WEAR A MARK OF SHAME UPON HER BOSOM.

A WISE SENTENCE! BUT IT IRKS ME THAT HER PARTNER SHOULD NOT STAND ON THE SCAFFOLD BY HER SIDE. BUT HE WILL BE KNOWN! -- HE WILL BE KNOWN!

HEARKEN UNTO ME, HESTER PRYNNE.

I HAVE STRIVEN WITH MY YOUNG BROTHER HERE, UNDER WHOSE PREACHING YOU HAVE SAT, THAT HE SHOULD DEAL WITH YOU, IN HEARING OF ALL -- THAT YOU SHOULD REVEAL THE NAME OF HIM WHO TEMPTED YOU TO THIS VILE, GRIEVOUS FALL.

BUT HE OPPOSES ME THAT IT WERE WRONGING THE VERY NATURE OF WOMAN TO FORCE HER TO LAY OPEN HER HEART'S SECRETS IN SUCH BROAD DAYLIGHT.

WHAT SAY YOU TO IT, ONCE AGAIN, BROTHER DIMMESDALE? IT IS OF MOMENT TO HER SOUL, AND, THEREFORE, MOMENTOUS TO THINE OWN, IN WHOSE CHARGE HERS IS.

EXHORT HER TO CONFESS THE TRUTH!

HESTER PRYNNE, THOU HEAREST WHAT THIS GOOD MAN SAYS, AND SEEST THE ACCOUNTABILITY UNDER WHICH I LABOR.

BE NOT SILENT FROM ANY PITY AND TENDERNESS FOR THE CULPRIT.

BELIEVE ME, HESTER, THOUGH HE WERE TO STEP DOWN FROM A HIGH PLACE, AND STAND THERE BESIDE THEE ON THY PEDESTAL OF SHAME...

...BETTER WERE IT SO THAN TO HIDE A GUILTY HEART THROUGH LIFE.

SPEAK OUT THE NAME OF THY FELLOW-SINNER AND FELLOW-SUFFERER!

WOMAN, TRANSGRESS NOT BEYOND HEAVEN'S MERCY! SPEAK! THAT, AND THY REPENTANCE, MAY TAKE THE SCARLET LETTER OFF THY BREAST!

NEVER!

IT IS TOO DEEPLY BRANDED! YE CANNOT TAKE IT OFF.

AND WOULD THAT I MIGHT ENDURE HIS AGONY, AS WELL AS MINE!

WONDROUS STRENGTH AND GENEROSITY OF A WOMAN'S HEART! SHE WILL NOT SPEAK!

DISCERNING THE IMPRACTICABLE STATE OF THE POOR WOMAN'S MIND, THE ELDER CLERGYMAN ADDRESSED TO THE MULTITUDE A DISCOURSE ON SIN, WITH CONTINUAL REFERENCE TO THE IGNOMINIOUS LETTER.

THE INFANT, DURING THE LATTER PORTION OF HER ORDEAL, PIERCED THE AIR WITH ITS WAILINGS AND SCREAMS; SHE STROVE TO HUSH IT. BUT SEEMED SCARCELY TO SYMPATHIZE WITH ITS TROUBLE.

WITH THE SAME HARD DEMEANOR, SHE WAS LED BACK TO PRISON...

...AND VANISHED FROM THE PUBLIC GAZE WITHIN ITS IRON-CLAMPED PORTAL.

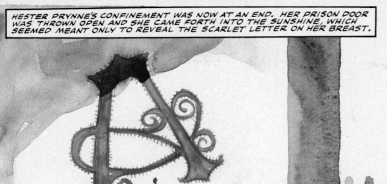

HESTER PRYNNE'S CONFINEMENT WAS NOW AT AN END. HER PRISON DOOR WAS THROWN OPEN AND SHE CAME FORTH INTO THE SUNSHINE, WHICH SEEMED MEANT ONLY TO REVEAL THE SCARLET LETTER ON HER BREAST.

IT MAY SEEM MARVELOUS, WITH ALL THE WORLD BEFORE HER, THAT THIS WOMAN SHOULD STILL CALL THAT PLACE HER HOME.

BUT THERE DWELT ONE WITH WHOM SHE DEEMED HERSELF CONNECTED IN A UNION, THAT, UNRECOGNIZED ON EARTH, WOULD BRING THEM TOGETHER BEFORE THE BAR OF FINAL JUDGMENT.

HESTER PRYNNE, THEREFORE, DID NOT FLEE.

ON THE OUTSKIRTS OF TOWN THERE WAS A SMALL THATCHED COTTAGE. IN THIS LITTLE DWELLING, HESTER ESTABLISHED HERSELF.

SHE INCURRED NO WANT, FOR SHE POSSESSED AN ART-- NEEDLEWORK. BY DEGREES, HER HANDIWORK BECAME THE FASHION.

HER OWN DRESS WAS OF THE COARSEST MATERIALS, WITH ONLY ONE ORNAMENT-- THE SCARLET LETTER.

THE CHILD'S ATTIRE, ON THE OTHER HAND, WAS DISTINGUISHED BY A FANTASTIC INGENUITY WHICH SERVED TO HEIGHTEN THE AIRY CHARM OF THE LITTLE GIRL.

HESTER NAMED THE INFANT "PEARL," AS BEING OF GREAT PRICE-- PURCHASED WITH ALL SHE HAD-- HER MOTHER'S ONLY TREASURE!

HOW SOON -- WITH WHAT STRANGE RAPIDITY INDEED! -- DID PEARL ARRIVE AT AN AGE THAT WAS CAPABLE OF SOCIAL INTERCOURSE. THE LITTLE PURITANS, BEING MOST INTOLERANT, SENSED SOMETHING AT VARIANCE IN THE MOTHER AND CHILD, AND REVILED THEM WITH THEIR TONGUES.

PEARL FELT THE SENTIMENT, AND REQUITED IT WITH THE BITTEREST HATRED THAT CAN RANKLE IN A CHILDISH BOSOM.

MOTHER AND DAUGHTER STOOD TOGETHER IN THE SAME CIRCLE OF SECLUSION FROM HUMAN SOCIETY.

AT HOME, THE UNLIKELIEST MATERIALS -- A STICK, A BUNCH OF RAGS, A FLOWER -- WERE THE PUPPETS OF PEARL'S WITCHCRAFT, AND BECAME SPIRITUALLY ADAPTED TO WHATEVER DRAMA OCCUPIED THE STAGE OF HER INNER WORLD.

THE PINE TREES, AGED, BLACK AND SOLEMN, NEEDED LITTLE TO FIGURE AS PURITAN ELDERS; THE UGLIEST WEEDS OF THE GARDEN WERE THEIR CHILDREN, WHOM PEARL SMOTE DOWN MOST UNMERCIFULLY.

SHE WAS ALWAYS DARTING UP AND DANCING, ALWAYS IN A STATE OF PRETERNATURAL EXCITEMENT. GAZING AT PEARL, HESTER OFTEN DROPPED HER WORK UPON HER KNEES AND CRIED OUT...

FATHER IN HEAVEN -- IF THOU ART STILL MY FATHER -- WHAT IS THIS WHICH I HAVE BROUGHT INTO THE WORLD?

OH, I AM YOUR LITTLE PEARL!

THOU ART NOT MY CHILD! TELL ME WHAT THOU ART, AND WHO SENT THEE?

TELL ME, MOTHER! DO THOU TELL ME!

THY HEAVENLY FATHER SENT THEE!

HE DID NOT SEND ME! I HAVE NO HEAVENLY FATHER!

TELL ME! TELL ME!

BUT HESTER COULD NOT SOLVE THE QUERY. SHE REMEMBERED--BETWIXT A SMILE AND A SHUDDER-- THE TALK OF THE TOWNS- PEOPLE, WHO HAD GIVEN OUT THAT POOR LITTLE PEARL WAS A DEMON OFFSPRING.

IT HAD REACHED HESTER THAT THERE WAS A DESIGN BY SOME TOWNSPEOPLE-- GOVERNOR BELLINGHAM WAS SAID TO BE ONE -- TO DEPRIVE HER OF HER CHILD. FULL OF CONCERN, HESTER PRYNNE SET FORTH FROM HER SOLITARY COTTAGE TO THE MANSION OF THE GOVERNOR.

THERE HATH BEEN MUCH QUESTION CONCERNING THEE-- WHETHER WE DO WELL BY TRUSTING AN IMMORTAL SOUL TO THE GUIDANCE OF ONE WHO HATH STUMBLED AND FALLEN.

WERE IT NOT FOR THY LITTLE ONE'S ETERNAL WELFARE, THAT SHE BE TAKEN OUT OF THY CHARGE AND INSTRUCTED IN THE TRUTHS OF HEAVEN AND EARTH?

WHAT CANST THOU DO FOR THE CHILD?

I CAN TEACH MY LITTLE PEARL WHAT I HAVE LEARNED FROM THIS!

IT IS BECAUSE OF THE STAIN THAT LETTER INDICATES, WE WOULD TRANSFER THY CHILD TO ANOTHER.

CANST THOU TELL ME, MY CHILD, WHO MADE THEE?

....

I WAS PLUCKED BY MY MOTHER OFF THE BUSH OF WILD ROSES THAT GROWS BY THE PRISON DOOR.

THIS IS AWFUL! A CHILD OF THREE, AND SHE CAN-NOT TELL WHO MADE HER! SHE IS IN THE DARK AS TO HER SOUL, ITS PRESENT DEPRAVITY, AND FUTURE DESTINY. WE NEED INQUIRE NO FURTHER.

GOD GAVE ME THE CHILD! HE GAVE HER IN REQUITAL OF ALL THINGS ELSE, WHICH YE HAD TAKEN. SHE IS MY HAPPINESS!--SHE IS MY TORTURE, NONE THE LESS! YE SHALL NOT TAKE HER!

I WILL DIE FIRST!

 MY POOR WOMAN,...

I WILL NOT GIVE HER UP!

SPEAK FOR ME! THOU WAST MY PASTOR, AND HADST CHARGE OF MY SOUL.

THOU KNOWEST WHAT IS IN MY HEART, AND WHAT ARE A MOTHER'S RIGHTS, AND HOW MUCH STRONGER THEY ARE WHEN SHE HAS BUT THAT CHILD AND THE SCARLET LETTER!

I WILL NOT LOSE THE CHILD!

LOOK TO IT!

THERE IS TRUTH IN IT. THIS CHILD OF ITS FATHER'S GUILT AND ITS MOTHER'S SHAME HATH COME FROM THE HAND OF GOD.

SHE RECOGNIZES THE SOLEMN MIRACLE WHICH GOD HATH WROUGHT, AND THAT THIS WAS TO KEEP THE MOTHER'S SOUL ALIVE AND TO PRESERVE HER FROM EVEN BLACKER DEPTHS OF SIN.

LET US LEAVE THEM AS PROVIDENCE HATH PLACED THEM.

YOU SPEAK WITH EARNEST-NESS.

INDEED, AND HATH ADDUCED SUCH ARGUMENT THAT WE WILL LEAVE THE MATTER AS IT STANDS, SO LONG AS THERE SHALL BE NO FUR-THER SCANDAL.

THE AFFAIR BEING SO SATISFACTORILY CON-CLUDED, HESTER PRYNNE, WITH PEARL, DEPARTED.

HIST! HIST!

IT WAS MISTRESS HIBBONS, THE GOVERNOR'S SISTER, WHO, A FEW YEARS LATER, WAS EXECUTED AS A WITCH.

WILT THOU GO WITH US TONIGHT? THERE WILL BE COMPANY IN THE FOREST; AND I PROMISED THE BLACK MAN* THAT COMELY HESTER PRYNNE SHOULD MAKE ONE.

MAKE MY EXCUSE TO HIM! I MUST WATCH MY LITTLE PEARL.

HAD THEY TAKEN HER, I WOULD WILLINGLY HAVE GONE, AND SIGNED MY NAME IN THE BLACK MAN'S BOOK TOO, WITH MY OWN BLOOD.

WE SHALL HAVE THEE THERE ANON!

*THE DEVIL

13

THE HEALTH OF THE TOWN HAD LAIN IN THE GUARDIANSHIP OF AN AGED APOTHECARY. THE ONLY SURGEON WAS THE BARBER. TO SUCH A PROFESSIONAL BODY, ROGER CHILLINGWORTH WAS A BRILLIANT ACQUISITION.

ABOUT NOW, MR. DIMMES-DALE'S HEALTH HAD BEGUN TO FAIL. THOSE ACQUAINTED WITH HIM ACCOUNTED FOR THIS BY HIS FREQUENT FASTS AND VIGILS.

THE ELDERS AND DEACONS WERE IMPORTUNATE THAT HE SHOULD SEE THE NEW PHYSICIAN. HE FINALLY PROMISED TO DO SO.

THE MYSTERIOUS OLD ROGER CHILLINGWORTH, THEN, BECAME THE PASTOR'S MEDICAL ADVISOR. THUS THEY CAME GRADUALLY TO SPEND MUCH TIME TOGETHER.

THE PHYSICIAN DEEMED IT ESSENTIAL TO KNOW THE MAN BEFORE ATTEMPTING TO DO HIM GOOD. WHEREVER THERE IS A HEART AND AN INTELLECT, THE DISEASES OF THE PHYSICAL FRAME ARE TINGED WITH THESE PECULIARITIES.

SO CHILLINGWORTH STROVE TO GO DEEP INTO HIS PATIENT'S BOSOM, DELVING AMONG HIS PRINCIPLES, LIKE A TREASURE-SEEKER IN A DARK CAVERN. FEW SECRETS CAN ESCAPE HE WHO HAS LICENSE TO UNDERTAKE SUCH A QUEST AND SKILL TO FOLLOW IT UP.

BUT, NOW, I WOULD ASK MY PHYSICIAN WHETHER HE DEEMS ME TO HAVE PROFITED BY HIS CARE?

SPEAK, BE IT FOR LIFE OR DEATH.

THE DISORDER IS STRANGE, INSOFAR AS THE SYMPTOMS HAVE BEEN LAID OPEN.

HATH ALL BEEN FAIRLY LAID OPEN TO ME?

HOW CAN YOU QUESTION IT? SURELY IT WERE CHILD'S PLAY TO CALL IN A PHYSICIAN AND THEN HIDE THE SORE!

A BODILY DISEASE MAY BE BUT A SYMPTOM OF SOME SPIRITUAL AILMENT.

YOU, OF ALL MEN I HAVE KNOWN, ARE HE WHOSE BODY IS CLOSEST CONJOINED WITH THE SPIRIT.

WOULD YOU THAT YOUR PHYSICIAN HEAL THE BODILY EVIL?

HOW, UNLESS YOU FIRST LAY OPEN THE TROUBLE IN YOUR SOUL?

NO! NOT TO THEE! --NOT TO AN EARTHLY PHYSICIAN!

WHO ART THOU, THAT DAREST THRUST HIMSELF BETWEEN THE SUFFERER AND HIS GOD?

WITH A FRANTIC GESTURE, HE RUSHED OUT OF THE ROOM.

A RARE CASE! A STRANGE SYMPATHY BETWIXT SOUL AND BODY!

I MUST SEARCH THIS MATTER TO THE BOTTOM.

IT CAME TO PASS THAT THE REVEREND MR. DIMMESDALE FELL INTO A DEEP SLUMBER.

TO SUCH A REMOTENESS HAD HIS SPIRIT WITHDRAWN, THAT HE STIRRED NOT WHEN OLD CHILLINGWORTH...

ADVANCED IN FRONT OF HIS PATIENT...

LAID HIS HAND UPON HIS BOSOM...

PULLED ASIDE THE COVERING...

AND GAZED AT THE GRUESOME MIRACLE.

THEN, INDEED, MR. DIMMESDALE SHUDDERED AND SLIGHTLY STIRRED.

AFTER A BRIEF PAUSE, THE PHYSICIAN TURNED AWAY...

BUT WITH WHAT A WILD LOOK OF WONDER, JOY, AND HORROR! -- WITH WHAT A GHASTLY RAPTURE.

AFTER THIS, THE INTERCOURSE BETWEEN THE CLERGYMAN AND THE PHYSICIAN, THOUGH EXTERNALLY THE SAME, WAS REALLY OF ANOTHER CHARACTER THAN IT HAD BEEN.

THE VICTIM WAS FOREVER ON THE RACK; IT NEEDED ONLY THE SPRING THAT CONTROLLED THE ENGINE -- AND THE PHYSICIAN KNEW IT WELL.

WHILE THUS SUFFERING UNDER BODILY DISEASE, AND TORTURED BY SOME BLACK TROUBLE OF THE SOUL, THE REVEREND MR. DIMMESDALE HAD ACHIEVED POPULARITY IN HIS SACRED OFFICE.

HIS POWER OF EXPERIENCING AND COMMUNICATING EMOTION WAS KEPT IN A STATE OF PRETERNATURAL ACTIVITY BY THE ANGUISH OF HIS DAILY LIFE.

THE PEOPLE KNEW NOT THE POWER THAT MOVED THEM. THEY DEEMED THE YOUNG CLERGYMAN A MIRACLE OF HOLINESS.

IT IS INCONCEIVABLE, THE AGONY WITH WHICH THIS VENERATION TORTURED HIM!

HIS INWARD TROUBLE DROVE HIM TO PRACTICES MORE IN ACCORDANCE WITH THE OLD CORRUPTED FAITH THAN WITH THE BETTER LIGHT OF THE PRESENT CHURCH.

IN MR. DIMMESDALE'S SECRET CLOSET, UNDER LOCK AND KEY, THERE WAS A BLOODY SCOURGE.

OFTENTIMES, IN HIS LONG NIGHTLY VIGILS, THIS PURITAN DIVINE HAD PLIED IT ON HIS OWN SHOULDERS.

ON ONE OF THOSE UGLY NIGHTS, WALKING IN THE SHADOW OF A DREAM, AS IT WERE, MR. DIMMESDALE REACHED THE SPOT WHERE HESTER PRYNNE HAD LIVED THROUGH HER FIRST HOURS OF PUBLIC IGNOMINY.

NO EYE COULD SEE HIM, SAVE THAT EVER WAKEFUL ONE WHICH HAD SEEN HIM IN HIS CLOSET WIELDING THE BLOODY SCOURGE. WHY, THEN, HAD HE COME HITHER?

HE HAD BEEN DRIVEN BY THE IMPULSE OF REMORSE, WHOSE SISTER IS THAT COWARDICE WHICH INVARIABLY DREW HIM BACK WHEN ON THE VERGE OF DISCLOSURE.

AND THUS, WHILE STANDING ON THE SCAFFOLD, HE WAS OVERCOME WITH A GREAT HORROR OF MIND, AS IF THE UNIVERSE WERE GAZING AT A SCARLET TOKEN ON HIS NAKED BREAST.

ON THAT SPOT, IN TRUTH, THERE WAS, AND THERE LONG HAD BEEN, THE GNAWING TOOTH OF BODILY PAIN.

WITHOUT ANY EFFORT OF HIS WILL OR POWER TO RESTRAIN HIMSELF, HE SHRIEKED; AN OUTCRY THAT PEALED THROUGH THE NIGHT.

IT IS DONE!

THE WHOLE TOWN WILL AWAKE AND FIND ME!

BUT THE TOWN DID NOT AWAKE; OR, IF IT DID, THE DROWSY SLUMBERERS MISTOOK THE CRY FOR SOMETHING FRIGHTFUL IN A DREAM, OR FOR THE NOISE OF WITCHES.

PEARL!

LITTLE PEARL! HESTER PRYNNE!

ARE YOU THERE?

HA HA HA HA HA

YES; IT IS HESTER PRYNNE!

WHENCE COME YOU?

WHAT SENT YOU HITHER?

I HAVE BEEN WATCHING AT GOVERNOR WINTHROP'S DEATHBED.

YE HAVE BOTH BEEN HERE BEFORE, BUT I WAS NOT WITH YOU. COME UP ONCE AGAIN, AND WE WILL STAND TOGETHER!

THE MOMENT THE MINISTER TOOK THE CHILD'S HAND, THERE CAME A RUSH OF NEW LIFE, POURING LIKE A TORRENT INTO HIS HEART.

THE THREE FORMED AN ELECTRIC CHAIN.

MINISTER, WILT THOU STAND HERE WITH MOTHER AND ME, TOMORROW?

NOT THEN, PEARL, BUT ANOTHER TIME.

AND WHAT OTHER TIME?

AT THE GREAT JUDGMENT DAY...

BUT, BEFORE MR. DIMMESDALE HAD DONE, A LIGHT GLEAMED FAR AND WIDE OVER ALL THE MUFFLED SKY.

SO POWERFUL WAS ITS RADIANCE THAT IT THOROUGHLY ILLUMINATED THE DENSE MEDIUM OF CLOUD BETWIXT THE SKY AND THE EARTH.

THEY STOOD IN THE NOON OF THAT STRANGE AND SOLEMN SPLENDOR AS IF IT WERE THE LIGHT THAT IS TO REVEAL ALL SECRETS AND THE DAY-BREAK THAT SHALL UNITE ALL WHO BELONG TO ONE ANOTHER.

?

WHO IS THAT MAN, HESTER?

I TELL THEE, MY SOUL SHIVERS AT HIM!

CANST THOU DO NOTHING FOR ME?

I HAVE A NAMELESS HORROR OF THE MAN!

BUT HESTER REMEMBERED HER OATH, AND WAS SILENT.

21

HESTER PRYNNE WAS SHOCKED AT THE CONDITION TO WHICH SHE FOUND THE CLERGYMAN REDUCED.

SHE HAD WITNESSED THE INTENSE MISERY BENEATH WHICH THE MINISTER STRUGGLED, OR, MORE ACCURATELY, HAD CEASED TO STRUGGLE. SHE SAW THAT HE STOOD ON THE VERGE OF LUNACY.

A SECRET ENEMY HAD BEEN BY HIS SIDE, AND HAD AVAILED HIMSELF OF THE OPPORTUNITIES TO TAMPER WITH THE DELICATE SPRINGS OF MR. DIMMESDALE'S NATURE.

HESTER COULD NOT BUT ASK HERSELF WHETHER THERE HAD NOT BEEN A DEFECT ON HER PART IN ALLOWING THE MINISTER TO BE THROWN INTO SUCH A POSITION.

HER ONLY JUSTIFICATION WAS THAT SHE HAD BEEN ABLE TO DISCERN NO METHOD OF RESCUING HIM FROM A BLACKER RUIN THAN HAD OVERWHELMED HERSELF, EXCEPT BY ACQUIESCING IN ROGER CHILLINGWORTH'S SCHEME.

UNDER THAT IMPULSE, SHE HAD MADE HER CHOICE, AND HAD CHOSEN, AS IT APPEARED, THE MORE WRETCHED ALTERNATIVE.

SHE DETERMINED TO REDEEM HER ERROR.

STRENGTHENED BY YEARS OF TRIAL, SHE FELT HERSELF NO LONGER SO INADEQUATE TO COPE WITH CHILLINGWORTH AS ON THAT NIGHT, ABASED BY SIN, WHEN THEY HAD TALKED TOGETHER IN THE PRISON CHAMBER.

THE OCCASION WAS NOT LONG TO SEEK.

I WOULD SPEAK WITH YOU.

AHA! AND IS IT MISTRESS HESTER THAT HAS A WORD FOR OLD ROGER CHILLINGWORTH?

HESTER WAS SHOCKED TO DISCERN WHAT A CHANGE HAD BEEN WROUGHT UPON HIM IN THE PAST SEVEN YEARS.

THE FORMER ASPECT OF AN INTELLECTUAL AND STUDIOUS MAN HAD VANISHED, SUCCEEDED BY AN EAGER, SEARCHING, ALMOST FIERCE, YET CAREFULLY GUARDED LOOK.

HIS SMILE PLAYED FALSE, SO DERISIVE THAT ONE COULD SEE HIS BLACKNESS ALL THE BETTER.

EVER AND ANON, TOO, THERE CAME A GLARE OF RED LIGHT OUT OF HIS EYES, AS IF THE OLD MAN'S SOUL WERE ON FIRE.

HE WAS STRIKING EVIDENCE OF MAN'S FACULTY OF TRANSFORMING HIMSELF INTO A DEVIL, IF HE WILL ONLY UNDERTAKE A DEVIL'S OFFICE.

WHEN WE LAST SPAKE, YOU EXTORTED A PROMISE OF SECRECY, AS THE LIFE AND GOOD FAME OF THE MAN WERE IN YOUR HANDS, THERE SEEMED NO CHOICE.

SINCE THAT DAY, YOU BURROW AND RANKLE IN HIS HEART. YOU CAUSE HIM TO DIE DAILY A LIVING DEATH, AND STILL HE KNOWS YOU NOT.

WHAT CHOICE HAD YOU? MY FINGER WOULD HAVE HURLED HIM FROM HIS PULPIT INTO A DUNGEON--

THENCE, TO THE GALLOWS!

IT HAD BEEN BETTER SO!

PEARL'S TENDENCY TO HOVER ABOUT THE ENIGMA OF THE SCARLET LETTER SEEMED AN INNATE QUALITY OF HER BEING.

THE IDEA CAME INTO HESTER'S MIND THAT PEARL MIGHT ALREADY HAVE APPROACHED THE AGE WHEN SHE COULD BE MADE A FRIEND, AND ENTRUSTED WITH A MOTHER'S SORROW.

"WHAT SHALL I SAY?" THOUGHT HESTER, "NO! IF THIS BE THE PRICE OF THE CHILD'S SYMPATHY, I CANNOT PAY IT."

MY LITTLE PEARL, THE GREEN LETTER ON THY CHILDISH BOSOM HAS NO PURPORT. BUT DOST THOU KNOW WHAT THIS LETTER MEANS WHICH THY MOTHER IS DOOMED TO WEAR?

NAY, MOTHER. IS IT FOR THE SAME REASON THE MINISTER KEEPS HIS HAND OVER HIS HEART?

WHAT HAS THE LETTER TO DO WITH ANY HEART SAVE MINE?

SILLY PEARL.

WHAT KNOW I OF THE MINISTER'S HEART? AND AS FOR THE SCARLET LETTER, I WEAR IT FOR ITS GOLD THREAD.

MOTHER, WHAT DOES THE SCARLET LETTER MEAN?

WHY DOES THE MINISTER KEEP HIS HAND OVER HIS HEART?

HESTER PRYNNE REMAINED CONSTANT IN HER RESOLVE TO MAKE KNOWN TO MR. DIMMESDALE THE TRUE CHARACTER OF THE MAN WHO HAD CREPT INTO HIS INTIMACY.

MOTHER, THE SUNSHINE DOES NOT LOVE YOU.

IT RUNS AWAY AND HIDES BECAUSE IT IS AFRAID OF SOMETHING ON YOUR BOSOM.

IT WILL NOT FLEE FROM ME...

FOR I WEAR NOTHING ON MY BOSOM YET!

NOR EVER WILL, MY CHILD, I HOPE.

WILL IT NOT COME OF ITS OWN ACCORD, WHEN I AM A WOMAN GROWN?

RUN AWAY, CHILD, AND CATCH THE SUNSHINE! IT WILL SOON BE GONE.

SEE!

I CAN STRETCH OUT MY HAND, AND GRASP SOME OF IT.

AS SHE ATTEMPTED TO DO SO, THE SUNSHINE VANISHED; OR, TO JUDGE FROM THE BRIGHT EXPRESSION THAT WAS DANCING IN PEARL'S FEATURES, HER MOTHER COULD HAVE FANCIED THAT THE CHILD HAD ABSORBED IT INTO HERSELF.

I HEAR A FOOTSTEP ALONG THE PATH.

I WOULD HAVE THEE PLAY, AND LEAVE ME TO SPEAK WITH HIM THAT COMES.

IS IT THE BLACK MAN THAT HAUNTS THE FOREST?

GO, SILLY CHILD! IT IS THE MINISTER!

WITHOUT A WORD MORE SPOKEN, THEY GLIDED BACK INTO THE SHADOW OF THE WOODS.

WHEN THEY SPOKE, IT WAS AT FIRST ONLY TO UTTER FRIENDLY REMARKS AND INQUIRIES: ABOUT THE GLOOMY SKY, THE THREATENING STORM, AND THE HEALTH OF EACH. THUS THEY WENT ONWARD, NOT BOLDLY BUT STEP BY STEP, INTO THE THEMES THAT WERE BROODING DEEPEST IN THEIR HEARTS.

HESTER, HAST THOU FOUND PEACE?

HAST THOU?

NOTHING BUT DESPAIR! WERE I A MAN DEVOID OF CONSCIENCE, I MIGHT HAVE FOUND PEACE LONG ERE NOW.

THE PEOPLE REVERENCE THEE, AND SURELY THOU WORKEST GOOD AMONG THEM! DOST THIS BRING NO COMFORT?

CANST THOU DEEM IT A CONSOLATION, THAT I MUST STAND UP IN MY PULPIT AND MEET SO MANY EYES TURNED UPWARD TO MY FACE, AS IF THE LIGHT OF HEAVEN WERE BEAMING FROM IT!—

—AND THEN LOOK INWARD, AND DISCERN THE BLACK REALITY? I HAVE LAUGHED IN BITTERNESS AND AGONY OF HEART, AT THE CONTRAST BETWEEN WHAT I SEEM AND WHAT I AM!

HAD I ONE FRIEND—OR WERE IT MY WORST ENEMY!—TO WHOM, WHEN SICKENED WITH THE PRAISES OF ALL OTHER MEN, I COULD BETAKE MYSELF AND BE KNOWN AS THE VILEST OF ALL SINNERS, METHINKS MY SOUL MIGHT KEEP ITSELF ALIVE.

BUT, NOW, IT IS ALL FALSEHOOD!— ALL EMPTINESS!— ALL DEATH!

SUCH A FRIEND AS THOU HAST WISHED FOR, WITH WHOM TO WEEP OVER THY SIN, THOU HAST IN ME, THE PARTNER OF IT!

THOU HAST LONG HAD SUCH AN ENEMY, AND DWELLEST WITH HIM, UNDER THE SAME ROOF!

WHAT MEAN YOU?

HESTER PRYNNE WAS NOW FULLY SENSIBLE OF THE DEEP INJURY FOR WHICH SHE WAS RESPONSIBLE TO THIS UNHAPPY MAN, IN PERMITTING HIM TO LIVE AT THE MERCY OF ONE WHOSE PURPOSES COULD NOT BE OTHER THAN MALEVOLENT.

O ARTHUR, FORGIVE ME! IN ALL THINGS ELSE, I HAVE STRIVEN TO BE TRUE! TRUTH WAS THE ONE VIRTUE WHICH I MIGHT HAVE HELD FAST, THROUGH ALL EXTREMITY.

SAVE WHEN THY GOOD- THY LIFE- THY FAME- WERE PUT IN QUESTION!

THEN I CONSENTED TO A DECEPTION.

DOST THOU NOT SEE WHAT I SAY?

THAT OLD MAN! THE PHYSICIAN! – HE WHOM THEY CALL ROGER CHILLING-WORTH!–

–HE WAS MY HUSBAND!

THOU LITTLE KNOWEST ALL THE HORROR OF THIS THING!--

THE HORRIBLE UGLINESS OF THIS EXPOSURE OF A SICK AND GUILTY HEART TO THE VERY EYE THAT WOULD GLOAT OVER IT!

WOMAN, THOU ART ACCOUNTABLE FOR THIS! I CANNOT FOR-GIVE THEE.

THOU SHALT FORGIVE ME!

LET GOD PUNISH!

THOU SHALT FORGIVE!

HESTER, HERE IS A NEW HORROR! CHILL-INGWORTH KNOWS YOUR PURPOSE TO REVEAL HIS TRUE CHARACTER. WILL HE CONTINUE TO KEEP OUR SECRET?

THERE IS A STRANGE SECRECY IN HIS NATURE. I DEEM IT NOT LIKELY THAT HE WILL BETRAY US.

HE WILL DOUBTLESS SEEK OTHER MEANS OF SATIATING HIS DARK PASSIONS.

AND I--HOW AM I TO LIVE LONGER, BREATHING THE SAME AIR WITH THIS DEADLY ENEMY?

THOU MUST DWELL NO LONGER WITH THIS MAN. THY HEART MUST BE NO LONGER UNDER HIS EVIL EYE!

THE JUDGMENT OF GOD IS ON ME. IT IS TOO MIGHTY TO STRUGGLE WITH!

BE STRONG FOR ME.

ADVISE ME WHAT TO DO!

THERE IS THE SEA! IT BROUGHT THEE HITHER -- IT WILL BEAR THEE BACK AGAIN. THOU WOULDST BE BEYOND HIM! AND WHAT HAST THOU TO DO WITH ALL THESE IRON MEN, AND THEIR OPINIONS? THEY HAVE KEPT THY BETTER PART IN BONDAGE TOO LONG ALREADY!

I AM POWERLESS TO GO! LOST AS MY OWN SOUL IS, I WOULD STILL DO WHAT I MAY FOR OTHER HUMAN SOULS!

I DARE NOT QUIT MY POST.

THOU ART CRUSHED UNDER THIS WEIGHT OF MISERY. LEAVE THIS WRECK AND RUIN. EXCHANGE THIS FALSE LIFE FOR A TRUE ONE! BEGIN ANEW!

O HESTER! THOU TELLEST OF RUNNING A RACE TO A MAN WHOSE KNEES TOTTER!

THERE IS NOT THE STRENGTH OR COURAGE LEFT ME TO VENTURE INTO THE WIDE, STRANGE, DIFFICULT WORLD, ALONE!

ALONE, HESTER!

31

Thou shalt not go alone.

Love must always create a sunshine, filling the heart so that it overflows upon the outward world. Had the forest still kept its gloom, it would have been bright in Hester's eyes, and bright in Arthur Dimmesdale's!

AS HE DEPARTED, IN ADVANCE OF HESTER PRYNNE AND LITTLE PEARL, THE MINISTER RECALLED THE PLANS WHICH HESTER AND HIMSELF HAD SKETCHED.

A VESSEL HAD RECENTLY ARRIVED, AND WITHIN FOUR DAYS' TIME WOULD SAIL FOR BRISTOL.

HESTER COULD SECURE THE PASSAGE OF TWO INDIVIDUALS AND A CHILD WITH ALL THE SECRECY WHICH CIRCUMSTANCES RENDERED DESIRABLE.

THE MINISTER FOUND THIS TIMING MOST FORTUNATE-- ON THE THIRD DAY FROM THE PRESENT, HE WAS TO PREACH THE ELECTION SERMON, AND COULD NOT HAVE CHANCED UPON A MORE SUITABLE TIME OF TERMINATING HIS CAREER.

THE EXCITEMENT LENT HIM UNACCUSTOMED PHYSICAL ENERGY, AND HURRIED HIM TOWNWARD AT A RAPID PACE.

AS HE DREW NEAR, HE TOOK AN IMPRESSION OF CHANGE FROM FAMILIAR OBJECTS. IT SEEMED NOT YESTERDAY, BUT LONG AGO, SINCE HE HAD QUITTED THEM.

IT WAS THE SAME TOWN; BUT THE SAME MINISTER RETURNED NOT FROM THE FOREST. NOTHING SHORT OF A CHANGE OF MORAL CODE IN THAT INTERIOR KINGDOM COULD ACCOUNT FOR THE IMPULSES NOW COMMUNICATED TO THE UNFORTUNATE AND STARTLED MINISTER.

AT EVERY STEP HE WAS INCITED TO DO SOME STRANGE, WILD, WICKED THING OR OTHER, WITH A SENSE THAT IT WOULD BE AT ONCE INVOLUNTARY AND INTENTIONAL; IN SPITE OF HIMSELF, YET GROWING OUT OF A PROFOUNDER SELF THAN THAT WHICH OPPOSED THE IMPULSE.

WHAT IS IT THAT HAUNTS AND TEMPTS ME?

AM I GIVEN OVER UTTERLY TO THE FIEND?

DID I MAKE A CONTRACT WITH HIM IN THE FOREST, AND SIGN IT WITH MY BLOOD?

DOES HE NOW SUMMON ME TO ITS FULFILL-MENT, BY SUGGESTING EVERY WICKEDNESS WHICH HIS FOUL IMAGINATION CAN CONCEIVE?

HE HAD MADE A BARGAIN VERY LIKE IT! TEMPTED BY A DREAM OF HAPPINESS, HE HAD YIELDED HIMSELF TO DEADLY SIN, AND THE INFECTIOUS POISON HAD BEEN RAPIDLY DIFFUSED THROUGH HIS MORAL SYSTEM.

HE HAD REACHED HIS DWELLING, AND, HASTENING UP THE STAIRS, TOOK REFUGE. HE WAS GLAD TO HAVE REACHED IT WITHOUT BETRAYING HIMSELF BY ANY OF THOSE ECCENTRICITIES TO WHICH HE HAD BEEN IMPELLED.

WELCOME HOME.

YOU LOOK PALE; AS IF THE TRAVEL HAD BEEN TOO SORE FOR YOU.

WE MUST MAKE YOU STRONG AND VIGOROUS FOR THE ELECTION DISCOURSE.

THE PEOPLE LOOK FOR GREAT THINGS, APPREHENDING THAT ANOTHER YEAR MAY COME, AND FIND THEIR PASTOR GONE TO ANOTHER WORLD.

HEAVEN GRANT IT BE A BETTER ONE. I HARDLY THINK TO TARRY WITH MY FLOCK THROUGH THE FLITTING SEASONS OF ANOTHER YEAR!

BUT I THINK I NEED NO MORE OF YOUR DRUGS, GOOD THOUGH THEY BE, AND ADMINISTERED BY A FRIENDLY HAND.

LEFT ALONE, THE MINISTER FLUNG AWAY THE ALREADY WRITTEN PAGES OF THE SERMON AND BEGAN ANOTHER, WHICH HE WROTE WITH SUCH A FLOW OF THOUGHT AND EMOTION THAT HE FANCIED HIMSELF INSPIRED.

THUS THE NIGHT FLED.

AT LAST, SUNRISE THREW A GOLDEN BEAM INTO THE STUDY, AND LAID IT ACROSS THE MINISTER'S BEDAZZLED EYES.

THERE HE WAS, THE PEN STILL BETWEEN HIS FINGERS, AND A VAST, IMMEASURABLE TRACT OF WRITTEN SPACE BEHIND HIM!

IN THE MORNING, HESTER PRYNNE AND LITTLE PEARL CAME INTO THE MARKET PLACE.

BUT SEE, MOTHER, HOW MANY FACES OF STRANGE PEOPLE, AND INDIANS, AND SAILORS! WHAT HAVE THEY ALL COME TO DO?

THEY WAIT TO SEE THE PROCESSION, FOR TODAY A NEW MAN IS BEGINNING TO RULE.

THE GOVERNOR AND THE MAGISTRATES AND THE MINISTERS ARE TO GO BY, WITH THE MUSIC AND THE SOLDIERS MARCHING BEFORE THEM.

SO, I MUST MAKE READY FOR ONE MORE BERTH THAN YOU BARGAINED FOR!

NO FEAR OF SCURVY OR SHIP-FEVER, THIS VOYAGE! WHAT WITH THE SHIP'S SURGEON AND THIS OTHER DOCTOR.

WHAT MEAN YOU, CAPTAIN?

ANOTHER PASSENGER?

WHY, KNOW YOU NOT THAT THIS PHYSICIAN-- CHILLINGWORTH-- IS MINDED TO TRY MY CABIN-FARE WITH YOU?

YOU MUST HAVE KNOWN IT; HE TELLS ME HE IS OF YOUR PARTY, A CLOSE FRIEND TO THE GENTLEMAN YOU SPOKE OF.

THEY KNOW EACH OTHER WELL INDEED. THEY HAVE LONG DWELT TOGETHER.

BEFORE HESTER COULD CONSIDER WHAT WAS TO BE DONE IN THIS NEW AND STARTLING ASPECT OF AFFAIRS, THE PROCESSION WAS HEARD APPROACHING ON ITS WAY TO THE MEETING HOUSE, WHERE THE REVEREND MR. DIMMESDALE WAS TO DELIVER THE ELECTION SERMON.

IT WAS THE OBSERVATION OF THOSE WHO BEHELD HIM NOW, THAT NEVER HAD MR. DIMMESDALE EXHIBITED SUCH ENERGY AS WAS SEEN IN THE GAIT AND AIR WITH WHICH HE KEPT PACE IN THE PROCESSION.

THERE WAS NO FEEBLENESS OF STEP, AS AT OTHER TIMES; HIS FRAME WAS NOT BENT; NOR DID HIS HAND REST OMINOUSLY UPON HIS HEART.

HESTER PRYNNE FELT A DREARY INFLUENCE COME OVER HER. HE SEEMED SO REMOTE FROM HER OWN SPHERE, AND UTTERLY BEYOND HER REACH. SHE THOUGHT OF THE DIM FOREST WITH ITS LITTLE DELL OF SOLITUDE, AND LOVE, AND ANGUISH, HOW DEEPLY THEY HAD KNOWN EACH OTHER THEN! AND, WAS THIS THE MAN? SHE HARDLY KNEW HIM NOW!

NOW, WHAT MORTAL IMAGINATION COULD CONCEIVE IT?

?

WHO, THAT SAW HIM PASS WOULD THINK HOW LITTLE WHILE IT IS SINCE HE WENT FORTH TO TAKE AN AIRING IN THE FOREST?

COULDST THOU SURELY TELL, HESTER, WHETHER HE WAS THE SAME MAN THAT ENCOUNTERED THEE ON THE FOREST PATH?

MADAM, I KNOW NOT OF WHAT YOU SPEAK.

FIE! DOST THOU THINK I HAVE BEEN TO THE FOREST SO MANY TIMES AND HAVE NO SKILL TO JUDGE WHO ELSE HAS BEEN THERE?

I KNOW THEE, HESTER; FOR I BEHOLD THE TOKEN. SO THERE NEED BE NO QUESTION ABOUT THAT.

BUT THIS MINISTER! WHEN THE BLACK MAN SEES ONE OF HIS SERVANTS, SIGNED AND SEALED, SO SHY OF OWNING TO THE BOND AS IS THE REVEREND MR. DIMMESDALE, HE HATH A WAY OF ORDERING THAT THE MARK SHALL BE DISCLOSED IN OPEN DAYLIGHT TO THE EYES OF THE WORLD.

WHAT IS IT THAT THE MINISTER SEEKS TO HIDE, HIS HAND ALWAYS OVER HIS HEART?

LAUGHING SO SHRILLY THAT ALL COULD HEAR, THE WEIRD OLD WOMAN DEPARTED.

BY THIS TIME THE PRELIMINARY PRAYER HAD BEEN OFFERED, AND THE ACCENTS OF THE REVEREND MR. DIMMESDALE WERE HEARD COMMENCING HIS DISCOURSE.

AS THE CHURCH WAS TOO MUCH THRONGED, HESTER TOOK UP HER POSITION NEXT TO THE SCAFFOLD. IT WAS CLOSE ENOUGH TO BRING THE SERMON TO HER EARS.

AND YET, MAJESTIC AS THE VOICE BECAME, THERE WAS FOREVER IN IT AN EXPRESSION OF ANGUISH...

...EVEN WHEN THE MINISTER'S VOICE ASSUMED ITS UTMOST BREADTH AND POWER, SO OVERFILLING THE CHURCH AS TO BURST ITS WAY THROUGH THE SOLID WALLS.

ITS VOLUME SEEMED TO ENVELOP HER WITH AWE AND SOLEMN GRANDEUR.

IT WAS THIS PROFOUND AND CONTINUAL UNDERTONE THAT GAVE THE CLERGYMAN HIS MOST APPROPRIATE POWER.

DURING ALL THIS TIME, HESTER STOOD, STATUE-LIKE, AT THE FOOT OF THE SCAFFOLD. THERE WERE MANY PEOPLE PRESENT FROM THE COUNTRY WHO HAD HEARD OF THE SCARLET LETTER, AND WHO NOW THRONGED ABOUT HESTER PRYNNE WITH RUDE AND BOORISH INTRUSIVENESS.

WITHIN THE CHURCH, THE HOLY SPIRIT COULD BE SEEN, AS IT WERE, DESCENDING ON THE MINISTER, POSSESSING HIM, AND FILLING HIM WITH IDEAS THAT MUST HAVE BEEN AS MARVELOUS TO HIM AS TO HIS AUDIENCE.

AND HESTER, AT THAT FINAL HOUR, WHEN SHE WAS SO SOON TO FLING ASIDE THE BURNING LETTER, FOUND IT HAD STRANGELY BECOME THE CENTER OF MORE REMARK AND EXCITEMENT, AND WAS THUS MADE TO SEAR HER BREAST MORE PAINFULLY THAN AT ANY TIME SINCE THE FIRST DAY SHE PUT IT ON.

WHILE HESTER STOOD IN THAT MAGIC CIRCLE OF IGNOMINY, THE ADMIRABLE PREACHER WAS LOOKING DOWN FROM THE SACRED PULPIT UPON AN AUDIENCE WHOSE VERY SPIRITS HAD YIELDED TO HIS CONTROL. THE ELOQUENT VOICE CAME TO A PAUSE. THERE WAS A MOMENTARY SILENCE...

IN A MOMENT MORE, THE CROWD BEGAN TO GUSH FORTH FROM THE CHURCH.

IN THE OPEN AIR THEIR RAPTURE BROKE INTO SPEECH. ACCORDING TO THEIR UNITED TESTIMONY, NEVER HAD MAN SPOKEN IN SO WISE, SO HIGH, AND SO HOLY A SPIRIT.

THE REVEREND MR. DIMMESDALE STOOD, AT THIS MOMENT, ON THE VERY PROUDEST EMINENCE OF SUPERIORITY TO WHICH INTELLECT, ELOQUENCE, AND A REPUTATION OF PUREST SANCTITY COULD EXALT A CLERGYMAN IN NEW ENGLAND'S EARLIEST DAYS.

ONCE MORE, THE RANKS OF MILITARY MEN AND CIVIL FATHERS MOVED ONWARD.

ALL EYES WERE TURNED TOWARDS THE POINT THE MINISTER WAS SEEN TO APPROACH.

THE SHOUT DIED TO A MURMUR, AS ONE AFTER ANOTHER OBTAINED A GLIMPSE OF HIM.

THE ENERGY--WHICH HAD HELD HIM UP, UNTIL HE SHOULD HAVE DELIVERED THE SACRED MESSAGE-- WAS WITHDRAWN, NOW THAT IT HAD SO FAITH- FULLY PERFORMED ITS OFFICE.

IT SEEMED HARDLY THE FACE OF A MAN ALIVE, WITH SUCH A DEATHLIKE HUE; IT WAS HARDLY A MAN WITH LIFE IN HIM, THAT TOTTERED ON HIS PATH SO NER- VOUSLY, YET TOTTERED AND DID NOT FALL!

AND NOW, ALMOST IMPER- CEPTIBLE AS WERE THE LATTER STEPS OF HIS PROGRESS, HE HAD COME OPPOSITE THE WEATHER- DARKENED SCAFFOLD, WHERE, LONG SINCE, HESTER PRYNNE HAD ENCOUNTERED THE WORLD'S IGNOMINIOUS STARE.

HADST THOU SOUGHT THE WHOLE EARTH OVER, THERE WAS NO ONE PLACE SO SECRET-- WHERE THOU COULDST HAVE ESCAPED ME-- SAVE ON THIS VERY SCAFFOLD.

THANKS BE TO HIM WHO HATH LED ME HITHER!

HE HATH ESCAPED ME.

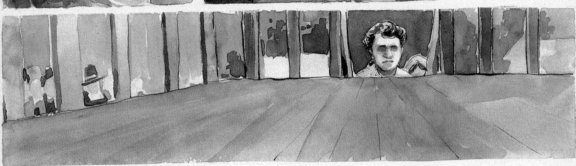

PEOPLE OF NEW ENGLAND! BEHOLD ME, THE ONE SINNER OF THE WORLD! AT LAST-- I STAND UPON THE SPOT WHERE, SEVEN YEARS SINCE, I SHOULD HAVE STOOD; HERE, WITH THIS WOMAN, WHOSE ARM SUSTAINS ME AT THIS DREAD- FUL MOMENT.

LO, THE SCARLET LETTER WHICH HESTER WEARS! WHEREVER HER WALK HATH BEEN-- YE HAVE ALL SHUDDERED AT IT.

BUT THERE STOOD ONE IN YOUR MIDST, AT WHOSE SIN AND INFAMY YE HAVE NOT SHUDDERED!

GOD'S EYE BEHELD IT! THE DEVIL KNEW IT WELL, AND FRETTED IT WITH THE TOUCH OF HIS BURN- ING FINGER! BUT HE HID IT CUNNINGLY, AND WALKED AMONG YOU.

NOW AT THE DEATH-HOUR, HE STANDS UP BEFORE YOU! HE BIDS YOU LOOK AGAIN AT HESTER'S SCAR-LET LETTER!

HE TELLS YOU THAT, WITH ALL ITS MYSTERIOUS HORROR, IT IS BUT THE SHADOW OF WHAT HE BEARS ON HIS OWN BREAST.

BEHOLD! BEHOLD A DREADFUL WITNESS OF IT!

FOR AN INSTANT, THE GAZE OF THE HORROR-STRICKEN MULTITUDE WAS CONCENTRATED ON THE GHASTLY MIRACLE; WHILE THE MINISTER STOOD, WITH A FLUSH OF TRIUMPH IN HIS FACE, AS ONE WHO, IN THE CRISIS OF ACUTEST PAIN, HAD WON A VICTORY.

DEAR LITTLE PEARL, WILT THOU KISS ME NOW?

AS HER TEARS FELL UPON HER FATHER'S CHEEK, THEY WERE THE PLEDGE THAT SHE WOULD GROW UP AMID HUMAN JOY AND SORROW, NOR FOREVER DO BATTLE WITH THE WORLD, BUT BE A WOMAN IN IT. TOWARDS HER MOTHER, TOO, PEARL'S ERRAND AS A MESSENGER OF ANGUISH WAS ALL FUL-FILLED.

SHALL WE NOT MEET AGAIN? SHALL WE NOT SPEND OUR IMMORTAL LIFE TOGETHER? SURELY, WE HAVE RANSOMED ONE ANOTHER WITH ALL THIS WOE!

HUSH, HESTER, I FEAR WHEN WE VIOLATED OUR REVERENCE FOR THE OTHER'S SOUL -- IT WAS THENCEFORTH VAIN TO HOPE THAT WE COULD HOPE TO MEET HEREAFTER.

GOD KNOWS; AND HE IS MERCIFUL!

HE HATH PROVED HIS MERCY IN MY AFFLICTIONS,

BY GIVING ME THIS BURNING TORTURE TO WEAR UPON MY BREAST!

BY SENDING YONDER DARK AND TERRIBLE OLD MAN TO KEEP THE TORTURE ALWAYS AT RED HEAT!

BY BRINGING ME HITHER, TO DIE THIS DEATH OF TRIUMPHANT IGNOMINY BEFORE THE PEOPLE!

HAD EITHER OF THESE AGONIES BEEN WANTING, I HAD BEEN LOST FOREVER!

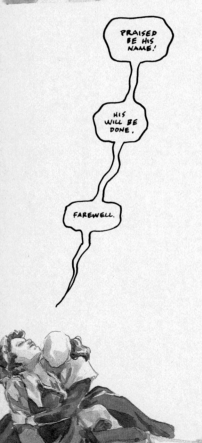

PRAISED BE HIS NAME!

HIS WILL BE DONE.

FAREWELL.

THAT FINAL WORD CAME WITH THE MINISTER'S EXPIRING BREATH. THE MULTITUDE, SILENT UNTIL THEN, BROKE OUT IN A STRANGE, DEEP VOICE OF AWE AND WONDER WHICH COULD NOT AS YET FIND UTTERANCE, SAVE IN THIS MURMUR THAT ROLLED SO HEAVILY AFTER THE DEPARTED SPIRIT.

Epilogue~

After many days, there was more than one account of what had been witnessed on the scaffold.

Most testified to having seen, on the breast of the unhappy minister, a scarlet letter -- imprinted in the flesh.

Some said he had inflicted a hideous torture on himself.

Others contended that Chillingworth had caused it to appear through magic and poisonous drugs.

Still others whispered that the awful symbol was the effect of the tooth of remorse, gnawing outwardly from the heart.

The reader may choose among these theories.

Almost immediately after Mr. Dimmesdale's death, Roger Chillingworth's strength and energy seemed to desert him.

At his decease, he bequeathed a considerable amount of property to little Pearl.

In no long time, the wearer of the scarlet letter disappeared, and Pearl along with her.

Years later, Hester Prynne returned, without Pearl, to where there was more of a real life for her than in that unknown region where Pearl had found a home.

She resumed, of her own free will, the symbol of which we have related so dark a tale. Never afterwards did it quit her bosom. But the scarlet letter ceased to be a stigma which attracted scorn and bitterness.

Rather, it became the symbol of her calling. Such helpfulness was found in her-- so much power to sympathize-- that people refused to interpret the scarlet "A" by its original signification. They said that it meant "Able"; so strong was Hester Prynne.

And, after many years, a new grave was delved, near an old and sunken one, yet with a space between, as if the dust of the two sleepers had no right to mingle. Yet one tombstone served for both.

On this simple slab, there appeared a herald's wording which might serve for a motto and brief description of our legend:

ON A FIELD
BLACK,
THE LETTER
'A'
RED

NATHANIEL HAWTHORNE was born in Salem, Massachusetts, on July 4, 1804, into a prominent Puritan family. Hawthorne's father died at sea in 1808, and his mother took to a life of mournful, eccentric seclusion and genteel poverty. As a youth, Hawthorne was well-read, concentrating on poetry and romantic fiction. In 1825, he graduated from Bowdoin College in Brunswick, Maine, and returned to Salem determined to pursue a writing career. While his early efforts were unsuccessful, Hawthorne's sinking spirits were briefly buoyed by the critical success of his *Twice-Told Tales* in 1837. To support himself, Hawthorne took a position in the Boston Custom House and accepted a number of writing and editing assignments, some of them hack work. He briefly edited the monthly *American Magazine of Useful and Entertaining Knowledge,* compiled *Peter Parley's Universal History,* and wrote a variety of children's books, among them *Grandfather's Chair* (1841), *Famous Old People* (1841), and *Biographical Stories for Children* (1842). In 1842, Hawthorne married Sophia Peabody, and settled in the countryside outside Boston to work on *Mosses from an Old Manse,* a collection of stories published in 1846. Still strapped for money, Hawthorne returned to the Custom House, where he worked for three years until he was discharged in 1849. Hawthorne then immersed himself in writing *The Scarlet Letter* (1850), which brought him immediate fame, and the popular *The House of the Seven Gables* (1852). He lived for awhile in the Berkshires, where he struck up a friendship with Herman Melville and labored on *The Snow-Image and Other Twice-Told Tales* (1851), *The Blithdale Romance* (1852), and two children's story collections. In 1853, Hawthorne became American consul in Liverpool, England, a reward for his work on a campaign biography of Franklin Pierce, the successful presidential candidate in 1852. He spent eight years overseas — five years as consul, and the remainder as a sightseer in Europe — before returning to Massachusetts, where he mined his European journals for *The Marble Faun* (1860) and *Our Old Home* (1863). Hawthorne died in Plymouth, New Hampshire, on May 19, 1864, while working on another novel. Portions from that unfinished novel and sections from his journals were published posthumously.

JILL THOMPSON was born in Chicago in 1966, and studied illustration at the American Academy of Art in Chicago. Thompson illustrated *Chronicles of Corum: The Bull and the Spear,* an adaptation of a work by fantasist Michael Moorcock, and contributed to *Strip AIDS U.S.A.*

P CRAIG RUSSELL was born in Wellsville, Ohio, in 1951. He received an art degree from the University of Cincinnati. Russell is known for his graphic adaptations of operas, including Wagner's *Parsifal* and Mozart's *The Magic Flute.* His credits also include illustrations for a version of Michael Moorcock's *Elric of Melniboné* and adaptations of Rudyard Kipling's *Jungle Books.*

YOU'LL NEED A GUIDE FOR LIFE'S GREATEST ADVENTURES!

Unbeatable reference books—exciting, easy-to-use, and always at the head of the class!

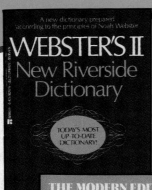

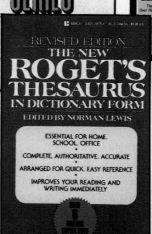

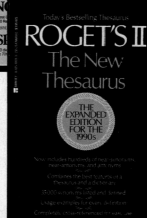